Mary Had a Little Glam

For Amanda Panda, #1 Fan. —T. S.
To Mommy, who always taught us to dress so well. —V. B. N.

ISBN 978-1-338-33167-7

12 11 10 9 8 7 6 5 4 3 2 1   18 19 20 21 22 23

Printed in the U.S.A.   40

First Scholastic printing, September 2018

The artwork for this book was created using Corel Painter, Adobe Photoshop CS5.1, and collaged vintage papers and fabrics.

Design by Andrea Miller

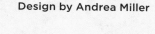

Mary Had a Little Glam

by Tammi Sauer

illustrated by
Vanessa Brantley-Newton

SCHOLASTIC INC.

Mary had a little glam that grew into a LOT.

And everywhere that Mary went,
she wasn't hard to spot.

But on the day she started school,
she caught some by surprise.
Sweet Mary shrugged and hugged her mom.
"I must accessorize."

Then Mary click-clacked down the block in **frilly** formal wear.

And by the time she got to school, she'd added extra flair.

MOTHER GOOSE ELEMENTARY

When Mary took a look around
her **heart** was filled with **woe**.
The other kids in class with her
were **glam-less**, head to toe.

So Mary offered fashion tips:
"More pink! More beads! More shine!

A hat for him and trim for her.

Go boa. It's **divine**."

Soon Mary brought out
glitz and *glam*
in everyone she met—

the students, teacher, principal, and Clark, the classroom pet.

Now story time had
gowns and **crowns**
and **mounds** of striped chiffon.

The art class came
with **glitter glue**
and trips to her salon.

Then Mary amped up music class
with **pomp** and **circumstance**.

At checkout time she was **sublime**,
left not a thing to chance.

The morning flew and soon it was
the best part of the day.
"It's **recess time**!" the teacher said,
and Mary led the way.

But all came to a sudden stop.
Each kid surveyed the scene.
**"We're clearly dressed
all wrong for this!"**
boo-hooed the seventeen.

Poor Mary twirled her parasol.
This crisis was a ten.
She'd never figure out a plan.
All was lost. But then—

She tossed her **shades** and **silk-lined cape**,
her scarf and **strappy shoes**.
And Mary's friends were just as fast—
there was no time to lose.

The class raced for the jungle gym,
the **spiral slide**, and **swings**.
Then Mary grinned and grabbed a ball
(among some other things).

Now Mary's flair for what to wear
is better than before.
True glamour often calls for lots . . .
But sometimes less is more!

Tammi Sauer is the author of many picture books, including *Chicken Dance*, *Cowboy Camp*, and *Your Alien*, which earned starred reviews in both *Kirkus* and *Publishers Weekly*. She is a former teacher and library media specialist who now celebrates reading and writing with thousands of kids each year through her author visits. Along with her husband and two children, Tammi lives in Edmond, Oklahoma. On occasion, they get a little glam.

Vanessa Brantley-Newton is a self-taught illustrator whose passion for children's books began when she came across *Snowy Day* by Ezra Jack Keats as a child in the 1960s. *Snowy Day* marked one of the first representations of black children in picture books, and seeing a character who looked like her and lived in a neighborhood like her own was a turning point in Vanessa's life. She hopes to inspire young readers as Keats did for her. Vanessa has illustrated more than 30 books, and is the author and illustrator of *Let Freedom Sing* and *Don't Let Auntie Mabel Bless the Table*. Vanessa lives in Charlotte, North Carolina, with her husband of 21 years, their daughter, and a very rambunctious cat named Stripes.